To

MW00532794

I hope This book
evokes memories. It's
our landscape as much
as it's Dinonnette's.
Love,
Rick

Following the Summer

Lise Bissonnette
Translated from the French
by Sheila Fischman

Following
the Summer

A NOVEL

Published in 1993 by
House of Anansi Press Limited
1800 Steeles Avenue West
Concord, Ontario
L4K 2P3
(416) 445-3333

First published in French as *Marie Suivait l'été* in 1992
by Les Éditions du Boréal

Canadian Cataloguing in Publication Data

Bissonnette, Lise
[Marie suivait l'été. English]
Following the summer

Translation of: Marie suivait l'été.
ISBN 0-88784-543-6

I. Title. II. title: Marie suivait l'été. English.

PS8553.I88M313 1993   C843'.54   C93-093590-X
PQ3919.2.B58M313 1993

Cover design: Brant Cowie/ArtPlus Limited
Printed and bound in Canada

*House of Anansi Press gratefully acknowledges the support of the
Canada Council, the Ontario Ministry of Culture, Tourism, and
Recreation, Ontario Arts Council, and Ontario Publishing Centre in
the development of writing and publishing in Canada.*

for Godefroy-M. Cardinal

Following
the Summer

A jet black dog, part basset, drags its round and tired body to the edge of the park. A thirsty day. Surge of men under scrawny trees. During another such July sulphur and wind paced out the area around the lake where a town would rise. With the first convoys that followed in the wake of gold or fraud. No man's land. *Around the borders a scorching yellow sun. Now the only hunters are singed dogs and children from the same brood. Above the anthills, invisible mists of Sunday.*

One

MARIE IS TWENTY YEARS OLD AND SHE is knitting, white yarn against a green bench. Click of needles, rustle of birds. Of birds she never hears, in this park that is suspended in dust. Birds pass in the distance, on the other side of the lake, as if they were tracing the exhalation of the mine. Breathing that reverberates close by, three streets in back of her, where a veil settles over the trees, invisible, but she sees it as grey. It's peaceful here, the leaves motionless, for the wind veers off at the first path, at the first dwarf trees, arrested in mid-growth as though someone has pruned them.

Behind the low wall the rumbling cars are silent now. It must be four o'clock because a shadow has stirred on the wide pool of moss, what is left of the spring. Green. She imagines herself as a young woman knitting and watching over a child in a park, in France, where urban roses bloom around rented chairs. Knowledge borrowed from books. As usual, it is the scent she cannot quite grasp, the sweetness to go with the ashes of this place.

At five she will go home, take back inside herself this nowhere city, this sultry day. A bag for her knitting, a leash for the dog, the hideous dog. Who for the moment has disappeared. Somewhere beyond the paved path, towards the trails, earth and bush, where curiosity used to draw her in the days when it still existed.

To the north, one branch of the path has been erased. As if no one wanders any more to the fences that protect the guest houses, the mine's castle-houses, now uninhabited for the most part. Though with their German casements and their French roofs they look as if they should be filled with servants: Their lawns slope down gently and stop at foliage that hides a glaucous beach lapped by the bile green of freshwater weeds. Poison.

The other path still follows the shore, gritty with sand and bald stone. This place was witness to her adolescent rage. Amidst the drought of trampled grass, the grime of furrowed earth, the acid ochre of rocks seared by the chemistry of the mine. Bright red beside the water, dusky rose between stunted blueberries sterile at the root, and littered cellophane, cigarette butts, torn pages of yellowed newspaper.

On another scorching afternoon a magic ceremony was held. Marie's glasses were used, with a sliver of sun, to set fire to the grass; she had entered the water beside the flat stone to immerse Isis, a cloth goddess. (Her terror, legs caught in the solid, acrid lake. "And if I fall?" — "Then you will decompose. — Rust." — "Shall I be reunited with gold?") It had taken an hour before Isis was dry, before she burned. "May those who stop us from leaving here be drowned or consumed," said Rita, her black hair the proper colour for casting spells.

Blurred ceremonies, and now only the colours remain. With nothing to do during this lull, Marie goes to look for her dog. She is near-beautiful and annoyed by a trickle of sweat on her face, by the sand that sneaks into her brand-new sandals.

She gropes for a place to step, her mind is blank, she is only impatient at being here, under this harsh sun, calling an animal. A clank of bicycles not far away, behind a knoll, punctuates the children's shouts. Husky voices, already coarse. The path disappears into higher grass near the top. She is exasperated.

A thin streak of half-dry clay, a square of shadow. Marie falls but it's nothing, only the sharp edge of a stone that makes blood flow at the ankle's hinge. A soiled dress, and now irritation because she must wait for the oozing to stop, beside water too dirty to use. No pain. Just a sense of absurdity, a spark of rage.

No, summers in this natural garbage dump brought neither rituals nor sorcery, neither revelations nor evil spells. Only the summer, as dull as this one, divided between cycling and forbidden dancing, between brief rainfalls and drought, between weekday boredom and

Saturdays when you counted the weddings. In the distance she hears the latest one, the blaring horns of rented Cadillacs, to be returned as soon as the wedding party has alighted at the hotel.

The dog has come back, has stopped moving. The animal has legs of unequal length, its eyes are reminiscent of ancestors we would like to disown, in photos where workers are dressed up like members of the bourgeoisie. Into dark suits and taffeta dresses with ruching are tucked the hardworking leanness of one, the fat of the other. Their hands give them away, as do the fixed stares of the children in their one pair of white stockings, eyes bulging at an everyday magic. The dog is panting like one of them, like the grandfather who every morning carted logs from his house to the workshop where he sharpened other people's saws and knives.

She is there to absorb it, along with the day's humidity, the dog's gaze. Nothing happens here, only scratches. A prison-land that drags its rocks like a ball-and-chain. Meagre shoots that lap up blood through the dust.

Go home now. The sun still harsh and high. Bicycles have delivered the children's cries to the rim of the park, to the little thicket of aspens, noon-hour stopping place during excursions, where they bite into thin bread, into ham grey with butter and light. Marie makes a final attempt to stem the oozing, now a paler pink. Behind her flits a brief shadow, scarcely more than a rustle on the sand-polished stone. Something like mockery in the voice. "Hurt yourself?"

Against the sun the lengthy silhouette becomes stocky, divided between the black slacks and the orange blouse. She's built like the grocer's wife, Marie thinks, straightening up. Her cheek brushes the slight curve of the other woman's hip. An ordinary woman, with sheep's eyes (like her own) and hair burnt by a cheap black dye-job.

A salesgirl, or rather a waitress in the beer parlour. When the town was finally populated there were twenty-nine taverns and ten hotels that children weren't even allowed to go near. The obverse of night, lights that turn the snow on sidewalks green, and ventilating fans that send out rancid odours, and in summer the sugary smell of beer. Whenever they walked under the awning of the Union Hotel (*Verres stérélisés, Bienvenue*) they laughed at the misspelled word. It was their way of showing contempt for the drunken midafternoon laughter that came through the swinging door. Laughter of people like this woman. You envisage them with sheets always rumpled, with unmade beds flanked by grubby night tables, with companions noisy and malodorous.

Her face is clean, her eyelashes thick. What is she doing here, on the other side of the lake? Does she not know the difference? Firmly, she grasps Marie's arm and shifts her to a higher position, leaning against a still-scorching rock. "You should be careful, it's dirty here." Takes a blue handkerchief from Marie (the kind you put in hope chests, that bring laughter from girls like her). "Could be dangerous, better clean it up right away."

A worn-out voice, one that's been hung up in many places. They have to be like that at night, mercenary, tolerant of alcohol and of jokes repeated a thousand times. Marie believes she can recognize them. Last year, on a day like this, she had tried to help to her feet a woman moaning softly in an alley, whom the police had taken to the station instead of the hospital. "Nothing wrong with her, she's dead drunk, she's always falling down, and when she starts chasing other customers away, the owner of the Royal kicks her out." As Marie signed the deposition, the human wreck stirred slightly, a howl of pain. The youngest officer had picked up the pale body covered with scrapes and tossed it into the station's only cell. Obscenities poured out in waves, as if the woman wanted their contempt. There was something enjoyable about being carried away by pity, about sniffing out the drama that had brought her here — desertion, or incest. No one could choose such abjection. Such dereliction, said the priest, who liked verbal precision. Marie was unmoved by dereliction, was only curious about the hoarse voice, so suited to curses.

The voice of this woman bending over her wound resembles the other, save for its oily slowness. She talks about rusty scissors, about scars that close over invisible infections, about abscesses and accidents that happen to children. Before Marie can even think about making her getaway, the woman spits gently into the handkerchief, turning it mauve, and wipes the wound, probing deep inside. Firmly, as if using a grater, she exposes the pink, she presses once again, and blood wells up, clean. Again. Marie's disgust is idiotic now, she knows that. Under the handkerchief tied as a tourniquet, the stickiness soaks into the cloth.

Go home now, quickly. Thank her.

The orange top exposes a plump elbow, rounder than her own. Like the arm that tucks you in on nights when you have a fever, tenderly, absently, already busy putting clothes away or turning off unnecessary lamps. "Thank you," says Marie, the routine words turning ridiculous. The dog shakes himself, stirs up the silence a little, but the woman does not move away. She walks with Marie to the edge of the park, supports her on the irregular stones ("I'm fine now, really, it's nothing"), and lavishes advice — Mercurochrome and cold water.

On the moss a man with tattooed arms has just stretched out. He pulls himself up on his elbows just long enough for the shadow of the two women to pass across his pale shirt. An orange blouse against a beige dress, dowdy now with its sober flowers, its (genuine) patent leather belt which matches the sandals exactly. Marie is a catalogue image with her carefully waved hair, her discreet earrings. Her gait becomes awkward. The other woman does not even see the man feigning sleep.

A crease of jealousy. Marie sees again Eleni, daughter of the Greek restaurant-owner who had the same confident sway when she brushed against the troops of boys in the narrow aisles at the arena. "*Love me tender,*" Elvis crooned, amidst the fine hail thrown up by their skates. Even in the depths of winter, when coats deform you and sweaters stiffen your silhouette, she still excited them. She had married the only West Indian in town and showed him off every night, dragging him down the main street, and there was no mistake. No possibility of mistake. She degraded every form of affection. And now a man stretched out in the park was using the same standard to judge Marie. Who didn't protest. Even regretted her innocent appearance under his shamelessly greedy gaze, regretted not wearing some violent colour that would drive up the bidding. A colour meant to be followed, to be summoned, as far as the rows of houses up there, that will protect you from consenting, from appearing to consent.

Neither the hour nor any shadow offers deliverance from the heat, the radiance. "I'm Corrine," says the other woman, her manner familiar. They slow down. Marie falls in with her heavy pace, the better to be filled with her odour of musk and sweat, which she should find repugnant. And which should enable her to keep her distance, exasperated, detached. Above all, not to be seen.

But none of this shows on the surface. The woman is thirty, at the very least. Her skin is dull. From the side, only her plump arms are visible, but her neck, observed just then, was somewhat crepey, her cheek chapped by the sun. Corrine is blind to Marie's disgust. She hears herself talking about three willow trees, the only ones in this town, with every passing season their bare roots more eaten away by the acids in the lake, trees that should be cut down. She talks about rot, about danger. Says on that score she knows what she's talking about, and laughs. An urgent generosity in her voice.

Marie sits on the grass that will crease her dress again. From her subservience it is obvious that she is pleading with the other woman to stay.

Two

ERVANT IS WORKING NIGHTS NOW, HE'LL punch in at nine p.m. This is the most difficult shift for surveillance of the blast furnaces, when everything operates in slow motion, when you're aware of the night inside the perpetual night of the blind building. He will need an hour or two of that numbness to stop feeling guilty for Marie's vexation.

There is no place for him in the drawn-out after-dinner hours. They passed him the bread, salt, fruit, then silence settled in behind the trivialities that engross Marie and her mother, two like voices that keep him at a distance while the father reads or dozes in the living room. It's about Ervant that they're talking, however, about the ceremony in which he will be the bridegroom, the other figure in the photographs whose settings they'll decide on tonight. From the radio come news items to which he pretends to listen, the coffee is too sweet. Marie could have done it deliberately, he's still the stranger here. The fiancé with no family, who must constantly be taken from the solitude of his rented room. He must learn how to say no.

He has ample time to read the hostility on the mother's thin, bare, faded lips after the meal. A quick dour look to question him, the same one she wore on the first day, the first night. She had gone to the basement, carrying glasses down, bringing others up; the party nearly over, the music dying away, conversations flagging, the girls already thinking of how they'd talk about it the next day. A lack of reserve in the gaze, a hand on the forearm, and she had guessed at her daughter's choice, Marie's choice: she would choose this tense and silent swarthy man who would not grow awkward with age as did the men from here. Curly hair like a child's, and dark. Laughing eyes, though, whose warmth, when it came, would make her daughter give way. A straightforward body.

There was nothing to use against him, except a measure of distance perhaps. He would never enter the house without knocking, his phone calls would be quick, a stranger's, coffee would be served him in a cup and saucer, he would never venture upstairs. His laughter was for some other place. In Marie's house there would be one last frontier, against the town which no longer resented these strangers who had in a few years become the law and custom of the streets. Yesterday in the mine, like Ervant, then business today, college tomorrow. Their homelands had prepared them for here, they were white and hard in the cold, they were lighthearted in pleasure when the summer nights grew long. Slavs from Central Europe, not even Gypsies.

The girls' mothers didn't really hate them. They only lamented the fact that their own sons went into exile, retracing the roads their fathers had taken, in the opposite direction, and that they were returning too late, after Marie, or Julie, had lost her initial fear, the provocative sharpness of unripe fruit, the brown slenderness of bogus Indians. And they married them, because the time was right for it, these immigrants whose sisters they will never know, with faces their own children will resemble one day.

An exact copy, only more incisive, of the history of these women who also followed immigrants from the interior, thirty years ago now. Thinking they were only passing through, they stayed, and Marie's mother is one of those who has regrets. Regret at having built a house, at having given her daughter a history that is so brief, so easy to repeat.

She no longer even tried to catch Marie and Ervant exchanging looks. Marie had long ago lost her reserve, and her mother was not one of those who spy at the front door when goodnights are said, who read diaries or sniff out the lies in accounts of last night, when her child becomes too talkative about new friends, when names are tumbled together the better to hide a single one. She didn't want even to guess where they might meet, in the little country house whose key Marie would sometimes ask for or, like so many others, near Powell's Hill for quick embraces inside a chilly automobile.

She knew her daughter inside out, especially in the shadowy zones. That Marie enjoys his body she has no doubt. But she understands her better at times like this, her keen, elusive bitterness. Which won't stop Marie from going out, from setting out with Ervant for a slow half-hour walk through town or the park, up to the fence around the mine, from taking pleasure again, becoming a little insistent, even, when they set the schedule for tomorrow.

Marie rises, doesn't even run a comb through her hair before she leaves, or take her purse. In the evening, not so acrid as the day because the wind has driven the smoke from the blast furnaces farther north, a smell of powder remains. "In this town it's a perfume," she says as soon as they've passed the corner, taking up a conversation from yesterday or before.

He learns all the mundane things about this place from her.

First they walk past the gas stations, separated here and there by a small grocery store or a snack bar. The hiss of the pumps, the creaking from shops with doors thrown open on the close of day, greetings shouted amidst banging doors, all this tumult is absorbed by the road that leads out of town, that you take here in the opposite direction. On either side the streets run uphill, with frame houses, some covered with brick paper siding and cramped together. Each is one or two storeys high and accessible only by steps, for the cellars open at ground level. Scraps of lawn, tufts of dried grass interspersed with dry earth, are strewn with bicycles, with that afternoon's toys. Apartment houses halfway up the slope fill the space between sidewalk and alley, houses already silent behind the narrow screens tacked to the bottoms of the windows for the brief days of heat.

On their right, finally, where the first curve of the lake appears, the schoolyard masks the entrance to the newer, richer part of town, where the waterside houses are made of real brick, with street-level entrances and garages that extend their length. You turn off before they come into view, then go down the two commercial streets, their businesses closed now, where the constant to and fro between taverns, restaurants, and movie houses continues to bring a little life. You can tell the older shops by their double display windows, which disappear into arcades. The more recent ones make a quicker impression, with their sidewalk-level facades and sometimes, on the richer ones, revolving doors.

The corner where the Paris Café stands, with its opaque green windows and its smell of French fries wafted outside by the fan, is the heart of the town. Teenage girls swap cigarettes, then go inside for another hour; young people go through the side door of the hotel across the street into the Moulin Rouge, where they'll drink for a long time, then dance in the violet light from faceted lamps. Life stops abruptly at the last traffic light, here where public buildings meet, the courthouse with its square wings cut from a monumental staircase, and the hospital on its high triangular plane, its cornices and windows in relief. It's like a resort before the bay of the lake, final indentation of the city.

This summer you must stay on the hospital side, for the walk along the bay is impassable, muddy, and strewn with rubble. In the arc of the circle that was once a beach stand the foundations of what will be a water-filtration plant, voted in long after the lake had been poisoned, long after the algae appeared, long after rot first showed up in the aspens. The building will be blind, and yellow, but that can't yet be seen. They walk faster now as they approach the only green in town, a narrow park that protects the most discreet neighbourhood, the one most restrained in its wealth, with stone houses of which only the pointed dormer windows, outlined in grey wood and roofed in copper, are visible over the hedges. They can be made out more easily if you skirt the park along the low stone wall, then go down one of the leafy lanes where they sleep, short streets that open abruptly onto the avenue that circles the mine.

You climb up towards the fence, letting yourself be swallowed up by the rumbling of the black mass that blocks the horizon, that breathes above the last dwellings, dilapidated ochre-coloured hovels whose joints are loose, all alike save for the yellow stucco of the last, with a windmill in front of it, barely a metre high. These houses are childless, made for the solitude of men come from afar, temporary mining cottages. Behind its windmill the last one looks empty, and they stop there, at the rim of the day-in-night created by the spotlights pointed at the railway that plunges inside the buildings. Locked up since it stopped receiving westward-bound passengers, the name of the station is Northland.

Marie knows nothing of what takes place on the other side of that fence. She was there for an hour, long ago, a school visit, and that was enough. All they'd seen was the cage, empty then, that the men would use later to travel up and down, and they'd walked through the neat and tidy control rooms. Ten minutes at most they could spend in the cavern of the blast furnaces, where coal-black human forms passed through walls of flames, holding long poles in their hands. Tightrope walkers seen from afar, as on a screen that eradicates terror. From high above flows golden lava that belea-guered eyes see as red. Men screamed who could not be heard, and in that inferno they were gods. On the platform from which they were observed, doors at either end opened on inner courtyards they fled to when their throats were tightened by the smoke, by the searing dryness of vats barely visible.

Is it gold or copper; she doesn't know. Of the inner mine she remembers just as well the gravelly places peppered with coal under a forest of pipes that link buildings with no name. This place is filled with the rhythmical rumbling that covers the town when all the others are silent. You can guess at the underground world and at the same time trample it. She has never tried to go back, especially since Ervant, who doesn't go near the fire, or doesn't talk about it to her: it's all the same.

The questions she asks are about the other place, about before, about the places he comes from, that he recreates for her.

Three

"T HE DANUBE IS DIRTY," HE SAID, "AND
Viennese men wear green hats."

His story about Vienna began long after the crossing
of the border, about which he was silent. It got under
way on Mommensgasse Street, at the corner of
Theresianumgasse, at the door of a boarding house, a
Gasthaus — the Gastwirschaft Zipler — which had
seven square windows on each of its four storeys.
Mornings he turned left and went to Julius Schöttner
Textiles, where half of the boarders were employed.
Evenings he crossed the street to the Maria Schneider
café, where there was no Maria and coffee only rarely.
The front entrance was that of a market stall, the bar a
former butcher's counter flanked by two tables, too
low, where Leonel, a Spaniard who worked at

Schöttner's, too, served nothing but beer. He was open from five until midnight, and silent between the two.

He lived alone with his young daughter, Fatima, who was eight years old, perhaps ten, and Ervant's story was rooted there, on the night he first noticed her shortly after his arrival at Zipler's. She was wearing a red sweater under the torn, faded dress he'd seen on so many women in the refugee camps — but of that, so near the border, he would say nothing. She went back and forth between the café and the Theresianumgasse, softly, like a cat in the sun, though coolness had long since settled in between the tall houses.

Meeting her on his way into the café, he felt the child's hand on his elbow, holding him back. Peculiar eyes, dark and too large under her heavy lids, a lamb's eyes that stopped the fall of a sparse fringe of hair. She wasn't beautiful, this city child raised on a diet of starches and dust, any plumpness of chin, cheeks, shoulders already gone. She plunged her old woman's gaze deep into the man's and made him lower his head towards her outstretched hand. She was begging.

From his jacket pocket he took a banknote and held it out furtively, guiltily. She took it, silently, slowly, ignoring the man's discomfort, and smoothed it with both hands so she could study it. He saw small rings, junky pieces that slipped a little on her fingers. He stammered a few words of German, asking her name. But she had finished and turned away from him. The red sweater was too big, it made a hump under her refugee's dress. Walking, she seemed to brush against shadows, then stood stock-still at the corner of the street, scrutinizing the evening's movements, no doubt hoping for some passerby.

The café door slammed, made him start before the cry from Leonel, whom he didn't yet know. "Fatima!" He heard it as "fatma," an Arabic sound, a female heaviness. But she was eight years old, ten at most, and he chuckled when he saw her answer the echo, then turn sharply without seeing him. All evening she sat near the bar, except when she went to the tables at a signal from Leonel to collect the dirty glasses that she'd wash in the back of the café. Clinking glasses, running water could be heard amidst scraps of conversation between workers who spoke different languages, who waited here for night. Around ten p.m. she left, at an order from Leonel.

That autumn was warm, and it took the Danube a long time to cleanse itself of the summer's filth.

Ervant was scouring the city in search of the youth of the world for which he had left behind stone roads, a roughcast village. He wanted glass, perhaps, or nickel, or wind that swoops into a corridor of concrete. But Vienna was living the new world in the old.

Around the Stefansdom, along the lighted avenues to which he often escaped, always alone, he gave no thought to the loden-clad men, the gloved women with blotchy faces who on the stroke of six swept into restaurants with frosted windows and restored wood panelling. Once, on a side street near the Opera House, he'd lingered at a table in a student café, pretending to read a newspaper that was held in place by an iron rod. No one paid him any attention, but he felt that he'd created some kind of sombre smell, here among the fair-haired young people who called out to each other with drawling courtesy. Sitting erect in a booth beside him, a girl had gathered her coat around her, marking her distance. He had gone outside, and the sound of his own footsteps on the cobblestones conjured up the sound of horses. There were none to be seen now, but their ghosts still hovered, over a vague stench of frying and the stone of imperial statues.

Eventually he found a place behind the cathedral, in a street of small hotels and movie houses. The blinking neon sign read WIMPY'S. The window came to the edge of the sidewalk, transparent over the row of red banquettes along which a boy in a peaked cap pushed a broom. Girls bustling behind the counter at the back wore pink boaters over hair pulled into a bun. The ritual was simple: the chime of the cash register, the posted menu with its numbered dishes, the plastic tray in its nickel-plated holder, the paper napkins, and the tables that were always clean. Near the one he selected were three short-haired young men speaking English, fast and loud, while huddled over a road map. Beside the exit an old woman in trousers, her back arched, sipped a Coca-Cola that she held aloft. She smiled at him over the waxed-paper cup. The broom creaked along the floor which seemed to be plastic, too. The light fell evenly over music that he didn't hear. Here he was free.

It was to this place that he brought Fatima, on the first Sunday they left the neighbourhood.

For the child had continued to accost him, at random, when there was no one to witness their meeting and she could still hold out her hand. A ritual of silence, to which he lent himself wholeheartedly, vaguely curious to see if she'd impose it on the others in the café, too. But he didn't know them well enough to ask, and above all he would have been afraid of putting an end to Fatima's little game. Sometimes he caught himself looking for her in the dusk of an empty street. A form, a being, a violence. Someone, in a word, who was not indifferent to him.

She never spoke, not even on the evening when they met some distance away, in the little square that dips down to mark the entrance to the Servitenkirsche. In any case they had no common language, and murmurs need time to acquire a meaning. It was raining, she wasn't even shivering, but still he ventured a protective move, a hand on her shoulder, and it nudged her onto the square in front of the church. The side door was ajar, she wanted to go inside, and immediately stood rooted to the spot before the mass of the confessionals, the twisted columns, the drawn curtains blocking the entrance to a baptistry, which was perfectly bare. He loathed churches, this one as much as any other: the side aisles with their padlocked grilles over blank-eyed Virgins or martyrs in their grimy tombs; the creaking of an old lady's chair, or the fearful rustling of a nun's habit — this one was counting the take from the candles while Fatima looked on, astonished; the brass plates of benefactors that celebrated their own death. Absences disguised as presences, so many lies amidst the lingering smell of cold incense and the humiliation of the kneeling benches.

A single rose-window cast its quicksilver light on the ageless statues, the plaster cones of paper flowers that marked the passage from one archway to the next. A Saint Sebastian carved in wood, as were the Stations of the Cross, hung from a column in the central nave, suffocated by the same flowers. Fatima dragged her creaking sandals across the false marble floor, slowly seeing everything there was to see. She touched nothing. But when the nun's headdress had disappeared she lit five candles. Resenting the viscous light that made the child as credulous as the women, he waited for her in the shadows, at the back. She returned to him with her impudent walk, she was out on the street before he could catch up with her. He had to go home by himself.

Then there was the castle, and the walk along the Danube. Fatima chose the places for their excursions, and he understood that she'd done so during the week. He became the guardian of longer escapades, of explorations. The castle was not a real castle but a big stone house dozing behind a high wall interrupted at either end by porte-cochères. The latches vanished under wall ornaments shaped like bunches of grapes, baroque reminders of some nouveau-riche splendour. One was broken, Fatima knew, and she waited for Ervant to push the heavy door. He did so without thinking, more sure of his abdication of will than of his curiosity.

Nothing happened. The courtyard was deserted, the gravel on the path poorly raked, and some dying ivy hung along the length of the servants' quarters, with their blind casements. Standing out against the horizon in a classical harmony as surprising as it was perfect, the central part of the house was invisible behind the truncated pyramid of its double staircase. When Fatima had satisfied herself by lightly touching all the entrances they sat down in shared silence, sheltered by the bannister.

Despite the acid autumn wind, the chill of the stone against his back, he was suffocating here as if he were in church, where objects were worn away, where fissures were worn smooth by worm holes and mildew, where flesh was everlasting marble. He wouldn't move, though, as long as Fatima was there, questioning a pediment, a cornice, or simply the space, which was suddenly carved out differently for her, accustomed as she was to streets in blocks, to public squares, to the unbroken rustle of the city.

She crouched on her heels just below him and he saw her from the back, her head more delicate now against her jutting shoulder blades. A father's thoughts occurred to him now, just as she was escaping him by not asking for anything. Cut her hair, dress her as a little girl in white smocks and Viennese lace, in dirndl skirts of flowered wool. But she lacked the slimness of his models. He could see a sharp elbow under the red sweater, a harshness that did not belong to childhood. He observed on her wrist a bronze metallic line, slender thread of a bracelet that stood out only faintly against her olive skin.

He took her hand, intrigued to find gold there rather than something nondescript made of glass. It was a perfect piece of jewellery, the clasp barely visible in the slim curved circle that clung to her wrist and moved so smoothly. He was sure he hadn't seen it before.

He gave her a questioning look, and she started to laugh, then gazed deeply into his eyes again with her old lady's expression. She unfastened the bracelet, made it dance, put it back on her wrist. Then brought her hand to her neck and started kneading some imaginary necklace. He thought he heard words in her laughter, a smattering of Spanish, but it was only the hiccups of an excited child, silenced abruptly when no echo came.

Their exploration of the castle was finished now; carefully he closed the porte-cochère, which would not engage, and they followed the brief maze of streets back to the square where they'd been just a short time ago. He didn't know why he was unwilling to walk with her to the café, perhaps because she herself took her distance before it even came into view. That Sunday she begged another banknote from him, before she disappeared, and he went off to spend his evening elsewhere.

The simplest of these October strolls had been their discovery of the path along the Danube. Ervant had gone there often, as had so many others like him who spent lonely Sundays in the city. There were no flowers, no fountains in their share of the border along the legendary river, where dreams no longer lingered as you drew near. From the paved walkway with its orderly rows of benches one could inhale the always pallid Viennese sun in a kind of natural prison: opposite, the tall grey masses of the first post-war homes, to the left and right, identical bridges, and behind him, the embankment wall of a railway line. The closer you got to the centre the more ornate the bridges became, the more the paths opened up. On Sunday, though, each person stayed inside his own perimeter, and the men from elsewhere watched time drift by in rhythm with the brownish water which carried with it the scum of urban algae and garbage. Around the pillars that supported the bridges, under a projecting wharf, the Danube became decay. But in spite of everything you stood watching, because all rivers go somewhere, and they keep you awake.

On Sundays around eleven o'clock, a man who rented bicycles opened his storage and display stand, setting up where the trains stopped. His only customers were young people who came here in groups and disappeared until nightfall. No sooner had Fatima come up to the platform than she was running towards the bicycles; they were too big for her and too heavy, but Ervant couldn't refuse her. They made a childlike racket between her falls and her victories on the machine, never leaving the square which was usually so quiet. She learned slowly, too often shaking with laughter, too often tense with fear, but eventually they arrived at an agreement, with brusque words they didn't need to understand.

With her dishevelled hair and red face, she looked her age. He took the bicycle back around four o'clock, she was beginning to shiver, and in the hand that now held his for the first time, on their way home, he felt the unembarrassed confidence of the smallest children when they get a head start on their sleep, when all they want from you is your presence.

He was very fond of her and thought he could rescue her from her world of bitterness. He extended their walks, introduced her to gardens and parks, to avenues and to iron gates laden with bronze birds. But she had regained her detachment and, when she left him, her eagerness. Wanting to astonish her again, to impress her, late one afternoon he took her all the way to the Stefansdom and the Wimpy's there that had become his haven.

At first she sat up very straight, well back in the restaurant booth, with her eyes half closed, her head like a dwarf's behind the table that was too high. Tidily she ate the near-tasteless hash that covered the rubbery bread, then ice cream in a cardboard dish. Facing each other, Ervant and Fatima were strangers again, resuming their silence, returning to the distance between a lonely man and another man's young daughter, a chance couple who seemed to have been placed there separately. Just now he regretted imposing himself, and he gazed with feigned abstraction at the paper streaked with pink, green, white, covering walls that looked freshly washed. She finished her ice cream while she took her own inventory of the place, her body suddenly alert, with the same hunter's tension she displayed at street corners near the café, when he ceased to exist.

He wanted to leave, but it was too late. Fatima had slipped away to the neighbouring tables and was exploring the three aisles with the same zeal she'd shown in the church. She had her own way of looking and at the same time ignoring. There was little life in the restaurant: two teenaged girls in identical black coats were sighing secrets to each other, a bespectacled man was huddled behind a newspaper, a few Sunday parents and children provided background noise around the remains of meals and cups of coffee growing cold. But he knew where she would stop, at the elbow of one of the three young men in bomber jackets who were leafing through magazines, absorbed in conversations that could only be about cars or music, in a syncopated German marked now and then by a Viennese languor. The first one to notice her was fair-haired, with the round folds of childhood bracketing his eyes; with a few laughing words he introduced her to the other two, who resembled each other with their muddy complexions, their open collars displaying the same chain, the same weak chins. She attached herself to them a few seconds later with such intensity that a brief silence settled over them, interrupted at once by the fair-haired one, who stroked her head.

Ervant thought her unsociable, but here she was allowing herself to be touched. It was too late to take her back, to understand, and he was unwilling to try. He grabbed her then and pushed her onto the street, ignoring the young people's sarcastic murmurs, anxious to get her back to the Theresianumgasse from which she would emerge again, or not, it was none of his business. The child was looking at him obliquely, she was beginning to yield. She was babbling now, something she'd never done before.

She kept him waiting at a stall on the edge of a laneway where an Arab immigrant sold newspapers and knickknacks from a box that he'd hide from the eyes of the police. Instinctively she had picked up the prettiest piece, a rhinestone necklace whose cheapness was cancelled by the purity of the setting, a circle in which the brilliance of the stones diminished regularly against some minuscule agates, black and regal. The two men barely debated the price, both of them eager for this day to end: it was six o'clock and the light was waning, leaving behind a cloak of dampness, the certainty, finally, of winter.

He crossed the Hofburg through the inner courtyard. A solitary guard stood watch at the entrance to the imperial quarters. He had thought vaguely of bringing her here, despite his loathing of the gilding of another era, and of wrinkles of every kind. He wouldn't do it.

They walked for a long time, as usual, through streets left empty by this first cold. The wind rose, whistling across the stones, and the chill rain of Vienna lashed down suddenly as they approached their neighbourhood. The public square for meetings, the Servitenkirsche. Outside the church they huddled in their new silence — bitter for him, terrifying for her — in their distance.

Still, she held out the necklace for him to hang around her neck, icy coals against the red sweater. There was a moment of tenderness as he lifted the hair of this thin young girl, made thinner by the rain. What would become of her? Already the tension in her neck, the defiant motion she had when she was hunting or lying in wait, had subsided into fear before this man who was leaving her now. He pulled her hair into a young woman's chignon and saw how heavy makeup, a broken oval, would make her ordinary by the time she was twenty, and he was sorry he had.

Gently he twisted her hair, the child's head on his hip. Night had fallen. Ervant was tall and warm in his wet clothes, and he felt Fatima's hand on his sex, firm, determined, the palm engaged at once in a back-and-forth motion that travelled to the root of his stomach. Night had come.

Four

A T THAT POINT IN HIS STORY HE TALKED about his sadness, then told how he had taken the child to the Maria Schneider café, right to the door that night, refusing to say goodnight in the hope that she'd understand her misbehaviour. A moral man, he felt indignant with Leonel, suspecting him of having taught his daughter that act, and others. Of having ordered her to beg, of having himself paid her in jewellery, the gold bracelet and the cheap ornaments, of having shown her how to offer herself. And of having left her for weeks with this solitary boy, for the money it brought her and with orders to seduce him should he become aloof. But Fatima was eight years old, ten perhaps, and Ervant's scenarios didn't always jibe with his recollections of that strange autumn, from which a little girl had emerged and then returned to the implacable silence of stone angels.

He had left Vienna a few weeks later, without going back to the café, without seeing Fatima again, though he watched her pass, up to her old tricks again, nothing changed.

When Marie heard the story she scarcely believed it. Especially that ending, left hanging. She imagined Ervant instead having surrendered to the child's strength, stiff, perhaps moaning in the hollow of that little hand that would have taken the time to slip inside his clothing, to rub the skin beneath the cloth, he would have encouraged her rhythm, his back against the wall and legs apart, then closed over the slender fingers and wrist, gushing in a slow, feeble spasm, just as he comes when she, Marie, caresses him standing against doors where he abandons himself in the daylight shadows of the empty house. She preferred the Ervant of agitation and suffocating heat to his cursing and self-pity, to his going home in the rain, detaching himself from a girl who was there to be taken, who was troubled and fiery, slave-girl with a necklace, the ugly girl who wins out over night.

And so she asked him no questions. It is he who would be surprised at her, at what seemed to awaken in her when he evoked the memory, so remote from those of his childhood in Odensk, to which she listened abstractedly.

Ervant preferred Marie bright-eyed and a trifle cold, the woman who had made him realize at once that his flight could end with her.

For after Vienna the only possibility was America, a final farewell to old stones, to homesick immigrants, to

misery always close at hand, and dusty shops that recreat-
ed an ancestral life. On the other continent there had been
no place for him; he had joined a group of midwestern
prospectors heading up to Canada, a frontier abolished for
the progress of mining, then gone on with some who
were on their way east, following a fault already exploited
and developed, where the French-speaking Klondike was
dying away. The houses weren't even thirty years old, the
girls even younger, and everything was hard like the
quartz that the rocks still yielded, pure, among the fallen
rocks in lands ruthlessly stripped of their forests.

From the radio poured western songs like those of
his first America, the cars were red or turquoise, with
aggressive fins, the two movie houses served up war or
horror, in English. He liked it all and cared little about
the other face of this country, one he could never com-
prehend because Marie had withdrawn from it. Here, it
was the other colonization, that of churches and the
land, which had grown insipid almost before the
church steeples were erected. She talked of it with quiet
arrogance, a hint of contempt in her laughter.

At the town limits where the paved roads ended, the
houses gave way as they did everywhere to burnt-out
areas. They went there together sometimes in the late
afternoon, because they'd found a seat carved from a
long bare rock, smooth and round, which offered a
view of most of the town as if it had been absorbed
into the distant sound of the mine. Near them, the ten-
nis court was deserted, behind a still-new convent.
Marie said little about herself except to declare that her
way of escaping was always through books, and that it

was easy. She described other scenarios for him, the stories of girls who were trapped.

There was Berthe who lived not far away, near Lac Edouard, which was no lake but the open sewer of a still-remote part of the town. People there were poor, the frame houses never lost their grey and their dust. Alone, she never went there, but when the nuns took their classes to confession, it was the shortcut to the church. Lined up in twos, identical teachers at the front and back, deformed by mantle and cowl, they grew bolder. The cold pinched them under woollen coats that were always too light, and they learned how to laugh at the first forbidden touches, gloved hands joined in coat pockets. Once caught they were separated, the fiat closing over this additional sin.

Berthe walked alone, at the back. Already recruited. They had enlisted her for their organ first, then for their devotions: drunk on incense, or to assume her guilt, eldest daughter of a drunk. The following year she would join them, veils to claw at her skin, brown soap and sour refectories. They had convinced her that ugliness lay behind her grim glasses and bushy eyebrows.

One warm spring day, when the smell around Lac Edouard was already turning rancid, the girls had laughed at the poor children, at the children of the poor who stood on their galleries, eyes filled with pain, a wheezing in their voices that echoed their mothers' cries. It was the last time before summer holidays and Berthe had stayed behind, hadn't come to confession, hadn't reappeared the next day or the next year. Marie thought she had died.

There was Madeleine, who lived next to the convent but didn't want it known, who was the first to arrive, the last to leave after the evening study period. A family whose children — no one knew how many — ran around with the dogs and pigs, near the stream that cleaned the stable. So it was said. For the presbytery was closed to them, as were the Church's good works, closed to these people from France who had no religion, whose daughter had been granted special permission to study at the convent, in hopes of conversion. With her almond eyes, her curly hair, her sun-tinged skin, Madeleine sowed hatred, love, and legends. She claimed to be the illegitimate daughter of the writer Colette, pointing to her name in the Index and showing them her photo as a bayadère; she claimed to be descended from the Porteuse de pain, still honoured by France for who knows what revolution; claimed to be the protégée of Ava Gardner, who would come to fetch her one day.

When Madeleine started to show, more beautiful than ever with a new, defiant way of holding her head, she too disappeared. Usually they laughed about these accidents of love, about the identity of the father, the sex of the child who would be born somewhere else. This time the whispers were as grave as terror, and virtually forbidden. In a cubicle reserved for the pianists, a fat girl close to the nuns had declared, under seal of a secret meant to be spread, that Madeleine had made the child with her own father, as her sisters had done before her, and that this explained the prolific inbreeding of the family who lived by the pigsty. Marie still wondered if it could be true, and why Madeleine was so cheerful.

"I had no friends," she said, hands joined around knees pulled up to her chin. She conjured up uglier girls who dreamed only of marriage, and more beautiful ones who dreamed only of marrying in English. She portrayed herself as an outsider who was heading down a literary path. She lied. She, too, had fed herself on romantic novels, on religiosity, on Madeleine's extravagant stories, on her own diary. She had made every concession. She had danced on her last day at the convent, in her white dress, this first elegance tarnished by the mechanic's son who had given her a wet kiss at midnight. There had been others, at the movies, at the Moulin Rouge. It was their ritual. She erased it now that it no longer had a meaning, now that she was convinced she had wiped out the pettiness of those days, escaped the triviality of that company of the feeble.

Because of Ervant, who was so unlike them. She got to her feet, looked down on the dark nape, thick like a labourer's, like labourers one doesn't marry. But he had a naked strength she never tired of. It was like rediscovering, at last, the first feelings of excitement, those she had forgotten, too: undressing at thirteen in the harsh hot grass, summoning the sun to the place between her legs, and waiting. Dampness, the corrosion of August.

Five

THE PEOPLE OF THIS LAND DON'T PUT down roots. They live where they can, along roads going north, between truck stops. They do not make gardens; they cover their houses with tarpaper, held in place by temporary laths. They wait, then they move on again, amidst the penury that clings to those who open the roads. That is why we know nothing about them. In the few photos kept by the priests are only the house fronts and streets turned grey by badly mixed acids. No adventurers' faces. The men standing outside their log cabins have expressions that apologize for their humility. Thus the grandfathers, washed up here by the Depression, came to this place by chance, chosen by the first masters. Later on they'll have wives, bashful women.

Legends have no faces here, no descendants, are like burned forests in which only aspens grow. Memories are short for children born so far away. In the attic, in trunks whose clasps are never locked, photos tell them of the marriages and deaths in families that will always be strangers, and they don't believe them. In cardboard cartons smelling of mothballs there are no lace handkerchiefs or jewels: only last year's rags and tatters, featherless felt hats, sweaters that will be unravelled one day, stacks of movie magazines, and a scrapbook of clippings about the English royal family. The children of this country are of their time, abridged.

Their knowledge of what is old comes from the abandoned houses they're allowed to explore on Sundays, when people go north in search of coolness, travelling along the colonists' old roads. Knees scraped on windowsills or cut by broken glass, or on torn-up carpeting. They found a family's castoffs, the wind whistled under a battered roof, a boy hoisted himself to the second floor despite the broken staircases. They found rusty hooks, a reader, a plastic crucifix, the head of an iron bedstead. In an old tool chest lay Isis, a brown wool doll dressed in a yellow leotard, a black crown pulled down to the eyes. At once she was a goddess, the Negro Queen of childhood, brought here from the back lanes of the town. They swore oaths to her.

And at the end of the summer they burned her. She had lost her powers, she was dead; to this country's children magic is short-lived. Marie, like the others, had agreed: it was time to temper their dreams, learn how to recognize them as soon as one had slipped inside. She

had destroyed the diary in which she had hated her mother, where she had run away, where she had copied out
sickly sweet poems. She had come to loathe this wasted
time. Isis had decomposed.

Six

ALL DAY LONG A GENTLE RAINFALL muddied the path around the future water tower. Summer mud snakes between scales of dried earth. Marie invents for herself an appetite for rain. Moves through it alone, though the sun, the extravagant sun, yesterday made her surrender.

Everything is so simple. The wound already closing, mauve under the bandage, the only oozing inside her body, in her private wetness, in a secret that is unimportant now. Everything so simple, inside a white raincoat.

Soon new titles on a bookstore shelf will offer a kind of deliverance. There are enough to last much longer than the week of night shift, which she always fills with American novels. Sentences that flow more slowly, words to be learned when they occur in the text, just as in the past, here in this part of the world, French was

learned by force, from Péguy's essays or the medita-
tions of Claudel. As for the American writers, Marie
confines herself to easy reading, the only kind of novels
that come here in any case, but they sometimes offer
images that please her: lonely bars, death that leaves no
trace, love in the afternoon.

The thirty-year-old bookseller has chin-length side-
burns, an intellectual's bony frame, and spectacles worn
over unfocused eyes. In the year that she has been seeing
him, for the two are always alone, he has never moved
from his safe place behind an old tailor's counter. He
barely greets her, lets her make her choice in silence,
and knows that soon she will consent to listen to his
slow monologues, in a language in which she dares
only to assent. "Why don't you try something else?" he
begins, never waiting for her reply. He won't wrap up
the yellow-covered books until he has plucked from his
piles of paper the latest issue of a gloomy magazine,
already dog-eared.

He reads slowly, one pale finger following the line,
paragraphs too weighty for her. He looks up: "Dreiser, I
say, Theodore Dreiser is what you should be reading
these days. I'll order a book for you, just one." She hears
the name, knows that he dreams of entering, through
her, the circuit that his other customers refuse him, only
murmurs neutrally, "From Europe?" Impatient or tri-
umphant, he purses his lips, bites into his reply with a
small sucking sound. She is his quarry for another fifteen
minutes, during which she offers only gestures, echoes.

Perhaps next week, she thinks, in the humid bookstore, hypnotized by his voice that is at once plaintive

and arrogant. Next week, perhaps, she'll give in.
Warmth encounters warmth and the window fogs over.
On ceiling-high shelves books lose their titles and
spines. The dark line of true reading. Take the yellow
novels in their paper bag and go. It is time.

She walks past shops that are closing one by one, the
rain a mere veil now, but the greyness has won. There is
the Europe of great literature, perhaps far away. But
there is Ervant's Europe, too, and it sometimes humiliates
her, drives her away. Last week, for instance, a day that
she hates to remember, when he arrived just after noon,
agitated, but with a look of triumph. With a package all
tied with string, something rendered shapeless by the
mail. Under stamps with foreign faces, Ervant's name
was capped with accents. The package had been
opened, then tied up again. "It's for you, from my mother," he said, excited. Did she remember that he had written his mother to tell about his life here and his future?
Had he told her, or had she heard him? Until now, the
mother had been just a shadow in a kerchief, left behind
in Odensk, a setting of icons, embroideries, a circle of
forests, once dark with murders, now with superstitions.
He mentioned it only to mark the distance once more,
to leave it again, break with it.

Marie saw Odensk differently, inaccessible to her. It
must resemble Montbrun, with its one road only slightly
wider at the church, then arriving at once at the woods.
Silent villagers, whose lives repeat themselves very early
every day, with pauses only for fatigue. Its women are
bent and always in skirts, and they make old things like
wax or soap, they beat rugs. There were no young girls,

and the reason for the men's exile was in that absence, even though Ervant had never said such a thing.

The package contained red slippers of imitation suede lined with plush, pointed like the footgear worn by ladies in hennins or by comic-book elves. The falseness of the fabric was obvious at once — the women there no longer wove, then, as they shivered by the fireplace — and these ridiculous slippers could be bought in the market.

Ervant smiled. And Marie liked only thin sandals or bare feet on carpets. She carefully folded the paper, uncertain whether to lie but already trapped. Pretend. Diminish. Dissemble. She questioned him about what he had written to his mother, to apologize for having become a daughter-in-law because those people knew only women who are cold. She must show this present to her mother, tolerate the murmuring, get through the sarcasm, hear herself whisper to Ervant how much she appreciates the peasant woman's kindness. And Marie was sure that he would smile again, shedding the discomfort of the man who had come here in ignorance.

That evening, the last one before the week of night work, she had escaped with him to the movies so she wouldn't be obliged to do anything more, to have a break before drawing out their time at the Paris Café, as usual. They had laughed, and she had let herself recover over brackish coffee because he knew a different way of talking. About the brass, the brown-gold Turkish coffee served there by every woman from the engraved pot she is given in the days of her beauty. They grow old in silence, in the presence of men, he says, and if he wants nothing of those women it is because they end up chattering among themselves, hating the daytime. He wants Marie with him in the light.

She doesn't know if she prefers this possessiveness, but it causes less pain than does affection in the guise of red imitation suede. She doesn't want his child: she simply wants him to close the door on her, to leave her frozen there and then awaken her. In settings they will devise together: sheets of satiny raw silk perhaps, a bed of unvarnished wood, a diamond-shaped vase on a low table, lamps that only faintly illuminate walls painted grey, walls painted blue.

Magazine images, which she confuses with intensity. She knows when it is five o'clock, as it is now, when the town goes home for supper, to kitchens that smell of vegetables and grease.

At a construction site, workmen are busy dropping canvas sheets over slabs of fresh cement, and one of them is whistling. He doesn't look at her. She hesitates where the two towns meet, near the hospital she has never been inside, hesitates between the road that follows the lake and the main street, at this unsettled hour when the street is emptying before its new activity begins, between the movie houses and the hotels. In this unaccustomed light of day the store fronts look greenish, and she feels unable to move, as in those dreams in which you're paralysed and objects are cast far away. Between the beauty parlour and Sally's Fashion, a distorting mirror makes her head longer, languid. She shakes herself, she's not one of those women who will push a baby carriage from street to street, from sale to sale, from season to season.

Of that she is certain. The bus-truck arrives from the north, by chance, and she is about to board it when she sees a woman come out the constantly swinging door of the Radio Grill, then knee her way into the restaurant next door. Under a red plastic raincoat the shoulders are square, it is she. And it's like listening to her talk. Marie tries for a closer look through the grease-streaked window that hides her now, but the bus driver, impatient, has started up.

She turns her back, sits on the long seat in front with two old women who will get off soon, at the old folks' home — it is already late — and she pulls her collar tighter. She is as cold as these old women probably are, who go from shelter to shelter. She has chosen to go home and that reminds her of the past when she would retch on her way home from Mass, moving from incense to the smell of roasting meat, having had nothing to drink but a long gulp of sun. Her nail polish is flaking onto her paper bag; the old ladies clutch their purses. Marie will disembark after they do, three stops later.

Seven

THE TREMOY ROAD IS FULL OF CARS draped with garlands, and on the only steps that cross the low wall a bride descends into the middle of the park. She is thin and glaucous, the hem of her gown droops around her ankles, stops at white stockings in low-cut ivory shoes. Rayon over nylon over satin, thinks Marie, an inventory of poverty; she looks for the bridegroom and finds behind the crinolines a little man squeezed into a powder-blue suit, with pleated lapels. She wishes them naked, against the ash tree where they'll be photographed, the girl lying on the mangy midsummer grass, her belly offered to the pigeons seeking company, the boy adding cigarette butts to those already lying around her satin shoes. The bodies of both would remain cold.

The dog salivates in his sleep, and grinds his teeth. Marie knows why she has brought him back here, why she sits in the same place, knows what she has been waiting for since the sun passed noon. The same warmth, the same understanding of things. The bridal couple will leave again, after exchanging fish-kisses, and it will be three o'clock, the hour when the day begins to wane.

In her black slacks again, and a flowered blouse with a halter neckline, Corrine has come along the Tremoy Road, too, and she is laughing. She bends over the drinking fountain, which is stained like a latrine, source of disease and forbidden to children, and the water that gushes up is almost silver. "Want some?" She presses the lever and it's an order. Marie hardly dares to hold back her hair as she slips beneath the other woman's shadow. Her throat is still dry, she has barely drunk, she all but trembles. Corrine laughs. "I've got something to tell you." As if she knew her. The dog follows. It's their first date.

They cross the park, leave its few patches of shadow, and go to sit on one of the sharp-edged rocks by the side of the lake, rippled today by an inner wind. They see seaweed swaying in a channel. Corrine asks how long she went to school and if she knows anything about depression. Marie says whatever comes into her head, it will do.

"My husband's in the hospital," Corrine says, as if talking about the seasons. She tells the story with no digressions, a composition in the style of advice to the lovelorn, and all that's missing is the solution. He's not really her husband, Pietro, an Italian, withdrawn but charming, she's been living with him for five years now, or a little less. They had a mobile home on the outskirts of one of those new towns up north where they first met, she was working in a bar, he on the completion of a road. The camps aren't what they once were, she explains, as if she'd known them all back in the days of the first workers' settlements, but she won't say anything about them. The men go down regularly to towns like this one, to join their wives and children and to putter around while awaiting their real return. Pietro was on his own, and they had agreed to make a life together by simple addition.

The small town had shut down, it happens, cobalt had been mined there and the market was bad. Corrine had persuaded him to move south, where she could find better-paying work, where they wouldn't be so isolated because the distance stifled her, sometimes. They'd moved into the second floor of the Union Hotel at a special monthly rate and hadn't budged. Every night Corrine went down to the main floor, behind the bar, and Pietro stayed upstairs, brooding and listening to the radio. He'd become strange, she said, a stranger, and so suddenly. He refused to look for work, he went out only at night when the noises down there had dissipated, he spoke only to her, to grumble about this place or to promise her another life, one that she did not care for, that would take them to the ocean, where he would play the harmonica in the sun.

Corrine was laughing again. "He's crazy, I know he is, but he's so good-looking." She was sure she could persuade him to stay here once he understood, and she sometimes thought they might buy the little movie theatre next door, where he could rule over all the dreams he wanted. She'd be the cashier and hostess, and they'd go on living late into the night.

But now he was smoking his nights away, one by one, while he waited for her to come upstairs.

Last Saturday, at the hour of waifs and strays, he had burst into the bar through the inner door. He saw that she knew them all, all these gaunt young men who were still funny and self-destructive, who would be reborn at noon, who kept Corrine hopping between the tables. She echoed them, she understood them, and they amused her. He left, walking past her, and she found him at dawn, two streets away, stock-still on the parapet of the old hydroplane dock. The lake was oily in the last heat of July. There wasn't room enough between them for the lapping of a wave or the death of a cicada. Yet he went on talking, piling up plans. They would go to the real south, to where the Gulf of Mexico resembles the area around Civitavecchia, there were plenty of places he'd know without a map, by instinct. He would build houses or repair the plaster of the haciendas, he would grow roses resistant to the scorching heat, he would plant fountains in schoolyards, all year he would drink fresh wine that she alone would serve only to him, he'd teach her how to roast sweet peppers, afternoons she would rest, to swell with child.

"I shut him up then. I said if I had a child I'd kill it." Pietro didn't say a word until the next night, he had swallowed a bottle of cheap sleeping pills, he was in no danger but she'd taken him to the hospital, to other stiflers of dreams, who would perhaps teach him resignation. She goes every day to see him, laughs at the white nightshirt that bares his hairy legs, she brings him cigarettes and he takes them as if she were clinging to him. He'll be discharged tomorrow. No one has asked what's wrong with him, only stammered prescriptions for rest to the plain-spoken woman he waits for and receives. In this country suicides hide in the woods, or succeed with a rifle. There is no contrition for refugees, for Italians who long for the sun, who cannot get used to shadows and beer. To warmth that is stored for the winter.

Corrine doesn't know what she wants from him. She says again that he's handsome, taller than his countrymen but more worn down, he is thin now, and dry like the tobacco he taught her to roll. Marie has never been inside the hospital but she can see the white before a boy's eyes, of the morning porridge, midday fish, evening stew, and the night that falls without music.

But Corrine is the one she understands, you don't make a child with a man whose plexus is elsewhere. You take them and you taste them. Marie has never known another hand between her legs than Ervant's, but she knows that strangers have a different way of touching, that they violate with reverence. Ervant tells her he once rubbed the clitoris of a woman who had stood off by herself, weeping, at a village fair, and that she came against his leg and offered him nothing in return. She knows that it is possible and that this woman's Pietro will lose her if he tries to unite their lives further. But it's not up to her to say so. The summer isn't over, she will come back to hear this story while protecting her own.

She wonders why Corrine never wears a dress, her black slacks are wrinkled at the knee and crotch, she looks like a waitress again.

Eight

IN AUGUST THE WOLVES DON THEIR SUNDAY best. Because she has no grandmother nearby and her mother knows none either, Marie doesn't know where she picked up this saying. But it comes to her at the approach to meetings that are never arranged, that are always kept, that bring her to the park near five o'clock. The grass is decaying from the sun, the dog is falling apart from arthritis and the heat, she holds on to her white knitting. The night shift now begins when the sun is still high, when Corrine goes back to the Union Hotel in time for the men's liquid suppers.

She has been taught beige, white, loose, she has learned parsimony in her choice of clothes for summers that are too brief. Corrine always looks different, squeezed into close-fitting blouses, skintight camisoles, slacks that fit tightly at ankle and hips, in blue, green, orange, in black streaked with red. She clashes with the grey rocks that they lie on. Marie avoids both the shade of the park and other people's looks at the two women, one of whom has neither purse nor dog nor necklace. On the flaking stone the sun is not so harsh now, the bicycles have disappeared, transgressing other boundaries outside the properties owned by the mine. The vast wrinkles in the solid dunes form hollow beds. They talk, Corrine always louder and longer.

Nothing about herself, or very little. Stories about people who live.

The big-breasted little prostitute who can't leave town because the morality officer reserves her for himself. She is in love with a college boy. She sets him ablaze in the early morning, he helps her make the bed and change the towels before her daily rounds. She is still pink and, already, absolutely alone.

The big bully who has refused to leave his room since his beloved returned to Montreal to go back to his wife and children. He weeps over a bag full of love letters and a fishing photograph that shows them with their arms around each other's shoulders.

A locksmith dressed in black from head to toe behaves like a curate in the face of bashed-in doors, yesterday's vomit, broken glass in the corridor. But he can be seen lingering outside those rooms where the new girls are always slow to awaken. He can get it up any time, any place, they say, as they leave him high and dry.

They all come from another north that can only be reached by the roads of the south, they've escaped from chapels and spider-mothers, except for the eldest

who is from around here. From the house with four
additions in back of the graveyard. Her mother was the
guardian of a mental defective whom she married last
June in white, in the church. The daughter followed the
priest's every move and spat at his feet before she
moved into the hotel, with no baggage. She is ardent
and insists on silence from her men.

Corrine knows nothing of the many forlorn men who
never venture from the upper floors, who welcome the
echo of bodies quick and drunk, sounds she pursues
when she goes to her room, that give her the urge to
make love. Pietro often turns her down now, and she
laughs angrily. She says it's like hunger: she feels wide
open and she must be filled, and she hates to do it herself. She leans across to Marie, still laughing. "There,"
she says, "and there." She has touched her pubis, her
groin. A burning inside the white cotton. Marie wasn't
afraid. And while Corrine is already at another story,
she parts her legs a little, invents for herself the memory of a woman she would have fucked, who will not
be. Strong, the stone beneath her back.

At the edge of the town's burnt-out area, that night
or another, they walked through the fence around the
former water tower. It was gaping. The building
hummed, they imagined the gurgling of pipes and
pumps, invisible through the series of filthy tiles on the
north side. Recumbent remnants strew the yard: a rusty
tractor, snow scrapers, tires, sheets of metal that may
have fallen from the roof. The water tower seems to
have a solitary life, to swallow its own refuse: they
brushed against it, whispering.

The entrance gave onto a bend in the lake to the west; it, too, was gaping. They had only to step inside. Machines gleamed, polished as if by a domestic sun, garlanded with vines, brushed by palms, by giant flowers that embraced their waists. All the green of the burnt summer was hidden there, now oozing the wet sweat of greenhouses inside a place of steel. The jungle opened out on two levels, darker inside the innermost recesses of the roof. Mist hauled itself along a blind wall, a serpent of fog that stopped at their feet. They were rooted to the spot. Everything sparkled under the white lights, even the cement floor painted silver grey, made to keep the dew inside and banish odours.

Corrine grabbed Marie by the elbow, spun her around to the right, to a recess behind a curtain of vines that clung to barbed wire. Lying on his back in a khaki hammock, a fat man slept. He was gasping, his face was waxen against a black sweater. The dog, tied to the fence, barked feebly. At a squirrel, perhaps, or a toad that had come with the calm weather. The women left.

Nine

I T APPEARS THAT THE ORGANIST RAN OUT screaming, that she tripped on the square in front of the church, that she took her time before telling it all to a child. A child who was slow to notify the firemen, on the other side of the Butte du Portage, who were playing cards in the shade, and there were those who claimed that one was asleep.

She wasn't playing the organ, she was drawing up the program for the choir at high mass, she was stacking the scores. Some claimed that she hung around the sacristy, where she had been found before, smoothing surplices and smelling the cold incense, unbuttoned and distraught. And it's true that her hair was loose, her collar open when they sat her down, hysterical, on the one bench in the presbytery yard, where the fire's progress could not yet be seen.

She had been stacking sheets of music, she said, when she heard a crackling sound that she thought was the struggling of a bird held prisoner in the vault. The sound left and returned, she saw nothing. And in the time it took to identify the yellow ribbon licking at the frieze above the staircase in the choir loft, the wall had suddenly burst into flames. She had always said it was unwise to decorate a church as if it were a living room, with frescoes painted on cardboard, flammable glue. For her, churches must be white as surplices, with plaster that would tolerate nothing but gold leaf. On her native island, which she never should have left, they had been made in that manner for three hundred years, and only the uneducated would decorate walls between stained-glass windows already crammed full of errors, secular intrusions like those poppies side by side with fleurs-de-lis on the rose-windows. She knew the church better than anyone, knew its smallest nooks and crannies, hated it in its entirety. And it was her possession that was burning.

Children were clustered on the sidewalk across the street, between the two hoses with inadequate pressure, the church having been built on the only hill in town. Now it is being consumed from above, a pyre in reverse, a witch whose brain would burn before her possessed body. One after the other the trompe-l'oeil gave way because their wood was dry. The arrow painted to look like silver, the first cornice painted to look like stone, the underpinning of the roof that had been painted like copper. Flickering fireworks blown towards the back, charred hunks of wood invisible in daylight. Now they're beginning to gnaw at the slates, false as well, that people always talk about replacing because their grey colour doesn't harmonize with the pale lemon siding on the walls. The ridgepole is burning all along its length, gleaming like a funambulist's wire, inaccessible to the streams of water, as though traced by a delighted god.

No alarm bell has sounded, but the crowd grows to watch the steeple fall, chimes of the poor that soon will shatter, in a puddle of water. It is a man, not the women, who is weeping now; they are busy herding the children out of the way. If he was the one who built the shell of the steeple, this is a sad business. But how can anyone know, the priest is on his annual journey to the Holy Land and the vicar won't return till late tonight from the far-flung parishes whose penitents require his presence once a week. The body, in any case, is burning more cheerfully now. And it's over, some brave soul has gone in through the basement to save the holy vessels and most of the objects in the sacristy. In the inferno, no one can see the vanished varnished pews, tomorrow only steel hooks will remain. It was a church without statues, and so with nothing to regret.

Marie climbs up the southern slope of the hill where the more opulent houses provide a view of the fire from a distance, in the event that the wind should drive it towards her. The summer has been so dry. But smoke and sparks continue to drift towards the back, near the grounds of the former boys' school, which is made of brick and empty now. Water is trained on the presbytery, trickles, cool, down the stucco, it will be saved.

She looks for sadness but finds none. The door had to be closed one day on the pale copies of the mystic emotions fostered in places like this, with their monotonous chants and promises of a peace as impracticable as it was offensive. She will only miss the giggles in the choir loft at the organist's trembling legs as she pumps away at the country harmonium. From up there, unless some lost soul blocked your view of the nave, you could see every detail of the twelve cardboard saints mounted on the walls, twice as large as life, some bearing the symbols of the evangelists, but most of them martyrs. All had the same face, the face of men-women indifferent to the flesh; they looked God in the eye and turned more pallid still as a result. Skeletons under the pastel robes. She will remember them more than the confessionals, though their terrors had more meaning, you entered them with your guts in a knot and left them a little less of a child, until you left them for good when there were other places to feel guilty in.

Her mother joins her by the fire, hypnotized for a moment. She has few memories in the rubble. It is the place where one enters a different age, from time to time. Women wore hats when she first came here, now they go bareheaded and soon her daughter was to be married there. The square outside the church is black with soot where confetti should have fallen. It is cement, it will survive, with enough room for the entire wedding party.

She sees Marie in the satin dress they've chosen, straight, short, with no lace. Only the back is to be bare and there will be no veil. A simple cap on her pulled-back hair, and pearls at the ears. A dress for a still-warm autumn, but able to defy the rain. It sleeps in plastic, it is perfect, it will always be.

Ervant will be upset. He rather liked this tacky church with its faint smell of northern mildew instead of old stones, wrapped in pastels instead of running, as it would have done in his country, into shadows propitious for women's moans. He had chosen the angle for the photo he'll send home, on the left where it would show the street and cars, including the rented convertible.

But now on the right a charred ruin stands, like a hotel that went up in flames one night because a drink was refused or a woman turned down. The steeple is a thousand pieces now and some people are gathering them up, already relics. Afterwards, next Sunday and on other Sundays still to come, the church will move into the old boys' school, so rumour has it.

Rumour has it, too, the following day, that the organist did not set the fire. That she had been in the sacristy, smoothing surplices. That the fire had been smouldering since the day before, that around midnight a neighbour had seen two shadows run away, shadows of a boy and perhaps a girl in a long beige car like the one that belongs to the sect with the crescent flag, which survives precariously somewhere near Bellecombe. Their children are brought to school by force and they refuse to kneel for prayer. In her class, Marie left them to their own people. She saw the mystery elsewhere, in their drawings of serpents and huts from which inner suns emerged. They came from the East.

Until the end of August, she goes by the Portage; every day a little more of its ruin has gone, leaving very little else. The ground is turning grey. Ervant is consoled, he studies the new houses. She goes to her appointments by way of the close-cropped knoll, she feels drained, she no longer knows how to come down.

Ten

THE DAYS ARE GROWING SHORTER FROM the middle. Marie's reason is restored from ten a.m. till noon, in the classroom where stuffy summer air lies stagnant despite wide-open windows. Traces of paste have been washed from the walls, the desks smell of bleach that never dries, textbooks are stacked in a corner, some will be left, there will be fewer children this fall. There's no exodus, says the principal who amends lists, refashions groups, and gossips from one class to the next. But the springs are drying up. The mine will soon shut down its underground development, nothing will be seen, the blast furnaces will continue to feed the chimneys. The men will no longer come. And the women who were born here will no longer provide. It will be September tomorrow, none of her colleagues is pregnant, they say that children are expensive but Marie hears summer creaking in their words. She's not the only one who merges with the rock, the crumbling clay, who goes by way of the dwarf aspens. Fate has brought them together.

And there's no other place to go. School, home, the park. If only there were a tavern where a woman could be alone in the dimness, to quench her thirst, to laugh softly at her ghosts, dispatch them in alcohol that really does dissolve them. What she knows about drunkenness is funny. Ervant taught her how to toss back vodka in one gulp, and you can see it clearly all the way down your back as you feel it go down. The table becomes solid, Ervant's shoulder, too; it's easy to start drawing a garden or living room furniture, a big living room like those in the new houses, in the addition to the old Townsite which has just been authorized. Easy to long for saucepans, china, silverware, and sheer curtains.

What she would see if she drank alone would be, perhaps, the road that leads out of here. Straighten its curves, repave it before winter, and soon you could save half an hour over the four hundred miles. She would drive, she would get there.

But at home there are only the sour wines her father cultivates in stoneware basins, that have to evaporate before they can be drunk; you don't sample them till winter, and then such a small amount.

From school to park takes twice as long if you go by way of the Portage. One last time Marie gives in, because it looks as if tomorrow there will finally be storms. She will draw out her walk along the main street, at least she can have lunch at Kresge's, alone and elbow to elbow with the old maids who watch the ballet of waitresses between the tubs of margarine, the production line of toast, the deep-frying vat, the coffeepot that starts up over and over. The place used to smell of breakfast all day long, it was the reward for hours of shopping on the Saturdays of her childhood. Unknown women in their thirties will certainly come here today, dragging their children to the stationery department just beside it. Strange plastic knapsacks have replaced flat bags this year, even leatherette has disappeared. There, hesitating over the schoolbags, will be a pupil destined for her class next week, whom she won't recognize once his mother shines him up. In her eyes they all resemble one another, despite what's said by those who like to think of themselves as pedagogues. You filter them through yourself as best you can, their affection is never sincere, no one is more duplicitous than a half-grown child.

The bookstore window has been changed, a new paperback collection she'll explore briefly, classics that she ought to tackle. But those can be kept for old age, a way to guarantee that you'll arrive there. Under its hardcover jacket the latest American novel offers the true story of a cold-blooded killer whose only motive is his hatred of quiet folk, of farmers and married couples. She takes it and the bookseller disapproves, she can tell from the way he gets rid of her.

She is alone at the outer limit of the park, with no dog or knitting, it's three o'clock, much earlier than usual, and if Corrine doesn't show up she'll be free of her, the interval will suffice, summer will have ended, a simple misunderstanding. Some willow leaves have already turned inside out, the storm will come slowly but it will come, before five o'clock, and then she'll have to run away at last.

She walks jauntily now. It wouldn't take much to make her feel the chill in the wind that is brushing against the rock at the edge of the park. From green and ochre, the poisoned water is turning black at her feet. Look, now the scar is a mere thread, not even wide enough to hold a secret. She wonders what colour the ice will be in January, when no one comes to this place where they dump the only old snow that is picked up in town, along the three commercial streets. Mauve, perhaps, like those plum-flavoured drinks that taste like artificial pectin. It's cheerful now, with the sun that plunges into the black water and does not resurface. You can resist all the lights come from elsewhere, make an opaque square for yourself and still be warm. She can't wait to read about the crime, that will be for Ervant's next night shift, the last one before the wedding.

Corrine isn't there, Marie would have to wait for an hour that she is wary of granting her. She advances firmly now, she knows every knoll, every patch of dried mud under the dead ferns, she will even walk by herself around the water tower whose fence seems to be permanently open. She wishes she could speak to the guard there, learn where he finds the cuttings and whether he knows all the names in his jungle. He is not like the foreigners, he has a belly and shoulders like those priests whose only abstinence is from women. Perhaps he too travels to the Holy Land, or to the

Christian Americas of the south, with their forests of perpetual rain. There is coolness between his machines, she will go farther inside it today, the water tower belongs to the town after all, it's not a private house.

Vapour falls almost in a mist as soon as she crosses the threshold, a great milky flower has burst on a stem that returns to the earth, she doesn't recognize it. An orchid, most likely, the only exotic flower Marie can recall, from a plate in some encyclopedia. Their names must be in Latin here, a mass of vowels that give even more grace to the green. There are palm trees that ooze a kind of oil, as if it was born from the vibration of the pumps.

And brief groans, a soft, regular hiss. She sees, then hears them. Underneath the hammock, directly on the cool earth, they breathe heavily with their exertions. The man on his back, stomach slumped across on either side, arms along his body, eyes shut, naked to the knees which are imprisoned by his clothes. The woman straddles him backwards, buttocks offered to his unseeing face, riding the penis that is visible down to the root, she is masturbating, her eyes howl. Her breasts sway inside the blouse she hasn't shed, a red spot where the sweat is darkening. There was wetness in her groan, she's coming hard.

She's finished before the man and now it's he who can be heard, she is making a spectacle of him for Marie, eyes locked on hers, contented. With both hands she spreads her buttocks, forcing him a little more, he comes in their mingled bushes. Corrine wipes herself with her underwear, unfolds herself, sways the hammock to fan herself, stretches, puts on her clothes. She is there, very close, closer even than the first time. Flings an arm around Marie's neck, plasters her sweat against her hips. "That was good, nice and juicy, I wouldn't mind starting over." Her loud laughter as she pinches Marie's thigh. "Come here."

The storm will wait until five o'clock on the rock where they lie to talk about flesh and folds. It is Corrine who says everything, Marie who learns. There are some men who give more pleasure, often those who sleep in strange places, who have no woman. You have to be able to guess who they are and be quick to take them. They laugh at his flaccid belly, his hissing groan. No matter, he is sleeping now, satisfied, and they are here and they've survived the summer.

A wave on the lake, then two. The rain will stop before their hair is even wet. Thunder booms, an Angelus.

Eleven

WITH THE MARRIAGE CAME AN EIGHT-DAY vacation. Marie would have liked to find a sea still warm in October, but Ervant had waited till fall so that he could finally touch New York in all its commotion, between seasons when his cousin who was lucky enough to live downtown had told him the weather was better. She quickly agreed because she also liked the hotels of novels, and she'd recognize those of New York, their windows always open to the sound of sirens. You made love there surrounded by the smell of other casual visitors, the rugs retain it, and the wallpaper next to the bathtubs. The doorman would whistle down a yellow cab, they never go to houses.

It was raining on La Guardia at dusk, and on the island of Manhattan where the first thing they found was the night. A torrent that lashed the embankment, that washed away graffiti from the overpasses. They drove across bridges to the accompaniment of wind-shield wipers, guessed at the tall cages of Harlem past 100th Street, then the private fortresses around the United Nations. There were no New Yorkers on the streets, iron curtains had been brought down across a thousand shops, not even a beggar on the corners. They didn't know what this desert resem-bled: they had never seen a full city, they'd wait for the taxi to stop. It pulled up in front of a hotel whose lighted sign was extinguished. The cousin had rec-ommended the Roger Smith Winthrop Hotel, he'd never been there because he lived in the centre of town, but it was just across from the side entrance to the Waldorf Astoria, where they were sure to see the best of what New York had to offer in the way of jewels and limousines.

The Roger Smith managed without a doorman and it opened directly onto a counter that was almost in dark-ness. The clerk was a thousand years old and as dusty as the pigeonholes from which he took a key, not look-ing at them: with just one suitcase, they could manage by themselves, the elevator was on their left. An ornate mirror sent back to Marie the image of a girl in a wrin-kled suit, it should have travelled better, but you bring the rain along with you. In the dim light Ervant was smiling, he saw only the succession of mirrors, he'd probably been afraid there would be old-style wood-work. Tomorrow, he said, we'll see everything.

A pretty room. There were many lamps, which broke up the mauve corners, the sirens howled their wonderful wet sound, the furniture was French provincial and there were floral prints and a writing desk that would make you want to write to Europe if you knew anyone there, because the Roger Smith provided stationery with its picture. A strange expenditure, since they scrimped on everything else, thin towels, thin bars of soap. Ervant wanted to go out, he knew all the places, including Rockefeller Center which must be quite close by. She declined, she wanted to fall asleep with something to look forward to, with the rain beaten back. To comply with the notion of a honeymoon she pulled him to her and opened herself to him. She knew he was thinking of tomorrow as he took her, thinking of the sun and sunlight on every window of every skyscraper.

They had forgotten to hang up the *Do Not Disturb* sign and to double-lock the door. It was half-past seven when the chambermaid came in without knocking; a voice apologized, then went away. As far as they could judge, since the room gave onto a high blank wall, the day would be grey and dry. The Roger Smith didn't offer room service and Ervant wouldn't have wanted it, he was eager to try the snack bar he'd spotted last night, its revolving door next to the elevator. Fresh butter on toasted white bread, coffee so insipid that they gulped it down, music stirring under the counter interspersed with an announcer's chatter predicting that the day would be mild. She understood every word and was surprised, it was the same English that was spoken around the mine, she'd never have thought it would sound the same. Ervant knew. They headed towards Rockefeller Center.

Ervant had drawn a map that started at the hotel and took in all the observation points, all the high places that would offer a view of the city. The contours stood out surprisingly well, although the day was grey. She cared little, in fact, about knowing exactly where the two rivers met, beyond the green mass of Central Park. His manoeuvres touched only the centre. He peered out through binoculars at the long avenues, spotted the most bustling places and decided on immediate destinations. He would never have enough of plazas where the only trees grew scrawny, in soil that looked more like asphalt. Of the summer there remained some strolling vendors of fresh-squeezed orange juice, office workers from the skyscrapers who went outside to wolf their plastic meals, the open air invective of escaped mental patients, and New Yorkers' taste for white cars, a sea of cars that seemed to fascinate him endlessly. He told her about life here as if he knew it, he didn't envy the rich, didn't look longingly in store windows. He dreamed of being swallowed up every day in the crowd that rushed to work as to a riot, through the inner mazes of the big buildings, insiders' shortcuts that he claimed to know. He covered the side streets, Grand Central took two hours, and that was where they stopped, in one of those cafeterias where trays are pushed at you before you even have time to read the menu. He laughed, he'd eat anything, even pastrami.

It took them two days to get near the park, some fifteen blocks from their hotel, and Marie made him walk there. He hadn't come here to marvel at the last flowerbeds that were lingering into October, or at the green that was only now turning to gold on low hills or in small valleys, or at scenes of mothers walking dogs along the southern paths, past the reassuring row of luxury hotels.

Marie would have liked to stay longer, to exorcise her memories of a summer that could never have occurred here, where you were never alone on a bench, where dogs must be kept on a leash, where the park opens onto the street, where if an unknown woman approached her, it would only be to ask the time. New York took its water from the big reservoir towards the northern tip of the park, a water tower would be impossible here, it would be padlocked. Here no one would be able to intrude. And she'd have liked to live here with Ervant, who would have been busy with something else. She'd have taught French to children who would arrive through the entrances on Fifth Avenue, she would come here at noon to read novels, perhaps even — finally — Theodore Dreiser.

Close to the deserted zoo, a young man stood over an old woman collapsed on a bench. He was dark-skinned with a poorly trimmed beard that frayed onto his thick neck, boots over jeans, a bomber jacket with metal studs. He was shouting in a foreign language, she moaned in reply, she had a flowered dress and legs covered with varicose veins, and she wore shoes with laces. In a flash he had struck her face, his anger soon vented, her moans even louder than before. Ervant was there at once, grappling the man from behind, shouting two or three words in the same language, then bashed him into a low wall. No one turned around, the old woman fell silent, Ervant was already dragging Marie towards the exit. The man wanted the money she sent over there, he explained, the people in his country didn't know how to behave in their misery. Ervant was irritated as much at the mother as at the son, you have to learn how to go away by yourself, you can always write, you shouldn't be surprised when the old people transposed here miss their other children. He knew every detail of their story, he pictured girls still young enough to go out bareheaded, standing outside the public wash houses, married to fearful village men, wishing they had the currency that would buy them sandals or delicate soaps. The evening was ruined in spite of the movies.

And the next day, too, because they had to visit the cousin and his wife, who were expecting them. They lived at 135 39th Street, between Third and Lexington. It was an ochre brick building with windowpanes surrounded by black metal like the ones you see all over the neighbourhood and that looked old to them. Air conditioners still wheezed on the upper floors, but according to the sign inside the door the cousin lived on the ground floor. The cautiously opened door, then the embraces. Only two connected rooms could be seen, the one window gave onto the yard and the back of the house next door, an iron grille lay crumpled across it, padlocked on the left. The janitor's quarters, and his cousin seemed to be happy here.

Ervant was tense throughout the meal, but he conversed willingly, she would never know about what. In English, she talked about her wedding and about New

York with the janitor's wife, a once-beautiful little brunette whose ravioli were excellent. She sewed at home and kept the hallways clean. There was wine on the table, in New York it costs nothing, and the lights were switched on around four. Ervant wanted to leave but first they had to tour the property, six floors and the perfect smell of bleach. All the doors had three locks, to which the cousin had the key, the corridors turned a corner to go to the apartments at the back, he'd put up mirrors so intruders couldn't hide there, to lie in wait for tenants. At the third floor they held the elevator for a young woman in glasses who was making fast all the locks on her door. She carried a heavy briefcase, she agreed with the janitor about when the exterminator should come, she had a French accent. Marie was curious but didn't dare speak, the janitor said she was subletting an apartment, he had no idea of her name. Washers and dryers in the basement, even when scoured the place smelled of grime, so the tenants preferred to take their laundry to the Chinese man next door.

When Marie and Ervant were finally outside again, the sun had broken through for the first time, a late-day sun that created lights for those floors that were still dark.

Now it was done, Ervant would no longer speak the language of janitors whom the new cities bury alive because they take refuge in neighbourhoods of the past. They didn't visit these places, only walked through them to the Village, where they wanted to go for the music. To hear jazz, he had no idea where, but they aimlessly followed a trumpet's moans. The musicians were white, the bar half empty, tourists, they were too early and Marie shouldn't have worn flat shoes.

An inexperienced singer leaned on the piano, a long golden skirt slit to the hips, wig-like hair a lacquered mass that fell to her breasts. The voice broke on lips smeared with pink, extended by a pencil to make them thicker. Marie slowly sipped a beer, they had no money for places like this. If they came back, she would at least consider wearing earrings, her red ones.

There was a gleam in the singer's eyes. She threw out her chest and offered herself to Ervant, the only man who was listening to her. Marie decided to enjoy it, leaned towards him to talk about the singer's wiles, to brush against him. But he was frozen there. His hand gripped his glass, his eyes locked on the woman's, she was undulating now. It was a waiter who roused him.

She expected more chance encounters like this one as they wandered the streets. On their last night they agreed to go to Oscar's, the Waldorf café, the least costly restaurant in the luxury hotel, where there were velvet banquettes. Ervant wore a tie, ordered wine with ease, dropped his discoveries one by one, talked about coming back. He even went so far as to tell the maître d'hotel that they were staying here, that they'd enjoyed their stay, that they had friends in New York. The man listened indulgently, he knew these refugees in search of plenty who came here seeking crumbs. He gave them better service.

Four women, noisy, came and sat at the next table. They weren't young, thought Marie, but their hair was like the singer's and their dresses were cut low. They were celebrating a divorce, telling each other salacious stories about the husband's impotence. The one with the reddest hair had her elbows on the table while she sipped her scotch, and Marie recognized the fleshiness of a Corrine. A woman who belonged in hotels. Ervant had fallen silent, was staring at these bodies that ignored him, was drinking in their throaty voices, sniffing the perfumes mingled with the sweat of late afternoon.

When I'm forty, thought Marie, he'll want me to bleach my hair and he'll buy me black underwear. I'll need heavy makeup the colour of no flesh that ever existed. My hips will be broad, he'll pat me on the rear.

She knew that she would arrange to grow old far away from him. She packed their bags at dawn while he slept, she still had years to leave him. Only the Corrines of this world were authentic, they are the only women who endure to the end of every summer, whose wrinkled hands make young men throw back their shoulders. On the eve of her wedding she had sworn never to see her again, the park would shut down when the cold came, there was no reason, she had lost her way. But the sirens screamed at daybreak. She would find her again, to learn.

Twelve

ERVANT HAD CALCULATED A THREE-YEAR WAIT before they purchased a house. They would live on one salary and stockpile the other. And postpone having children until they possessed a back yard. Their three-room apartment in one of the first blocks to go up behind the hospital would be furnished sparsely while they waited. To the west the windows looked out on the first slope of a hill, on bare trees. They hadn't had time to eat on the balcony even once before the first sudden showers. Everything shut properly, the closet doors as well as the one to the landing. They could hear nothing and Ervant could turn up the stereo and the TV set, which he liked to have on at all times.

He no longer worked nights. He'd moved up to the surface, to conveyor-belt maintenance. When Marie went home in the middle of the day she missed him.

The white sun in the warm bedroom was made for Ervant, so playful when he made love. He laughed in what he said was the language of cats, clawing faintly, and he could come just like that while looking into her eyes. Evenings, they had to talk a little more, find ways to understand each other. With a key now, and a mail-box in his name, he was able to shake off his memories. Already conversations sprang from something else, from school, the mine, the newspaper, often from TV series. Early dark, the swift passage of time.

She had little time to look for Corrine, but she knew she must. In class a dark-haired twelve-year-old girl stared at her with the same eyes, slightly protruding and obstinate, in a face made red by cold houses. For once Marie took an interest in a pupil, even though she was without talent. Who talked fast, gave orders, wrote dirty words in English on the board, and pushed around the younger, timid pupils. Marie had seized an illustrated pornographic book that lay open on her desk, a European publication brought here through some chain of forlorn nomads. The child had faltered. Her splendid arrogance was gone now, and from quivering lips came a faded voice. "It's my father's . . ." Her fear passed like a sudden chill. Marie had pictured a violent father, a pleasure-seeker from whom the daughter had stolen a secret. She had taken pity and heard herself simply ask the girl to leave the book at home. She had said thanks, and in her mouth the word sounded like one in a foreign language. Her name was Diane, though, like other local girls.

One late November evening a violent rainstorm froze the snow that had fallen the day before. People walked on the road, where the ruts iced over more slowly. There, not far from the school, she saw Diane walking — alone, bareheaded, already soaking wet. She followed her for a while, a small form with hunched shoulders whom a car could have swept away like a wisp of straw. A little slip of a thing. Marie's umbrella was red, more easily visible. She took the girl's hand and went two or three blocks with her. Her palm was as cold as her fingers, what was the terror that filled this child? She wanted to walk her home, but Diane stopped to take her leave at the corner by the Protestant school. A streetlamp lit the deserted schoolyard. Marie saw a face puffy with tears, heard the beginning of a hiccup. A second later, perhaps two, and Diane had gone. She saw her fall on Pinder hill, get up, pause, probably swallowing, then climb up the stairs of one of those square blocks stacked with Depression-era apartments. Their musty smell touched even the people who lived there.

First thing the next day, Diane was swaggering. During the prayer that was read over the intercom she had unbuttoned her collar to show the two big girls behind her something that made them giggle. At recess she showed the little girls what she called love bites, two perfect bruises at the top of her barely formed breasts, and explained to them how a boy can give them to a girl. She claimed to have met one the night before, a friend of her brother's, who had left them alone. She laughed and continued to tell her story until Marie could hear her, so that she could hear her.

Later that day, when she expressed her concern, a colleague said that some months ago Diane's father had been accused of incest and released for lack of evidence. The mother had gone away, no one knew where. And Diane was constantly proclaiming her admiration for the man who was, apparently, very handsome. The colleague turned away. "You'll have all kinds of suspicions," he said, "but you won't be able to do a thing. Just stay calm." She was on the lookout though, ready to respond to the smallest sign of distress. There were none. Perhaps after all she'd confused tears with rain, silence with refusal. Diane was robust and insolent, she masterminded the minor disturbances of the day, and she was the first to disappear when school was over.

At best, thought Marie, she'll turn out to be a Corrine. The drama, if there is one, would vanish with what remained of her childhood. And she had enough of the toughness needed to keep her distance from any torments, to take from others the scrap of life that had been snatched away from her. When she turned sixteen, unless some priest got mixed up in it, the father would be just another man among men, and Diane would have restored to her once again laughter come in from the cold. A survivor, a thistle.

The frost had settled in, but through this child-woman with her tarnished gaze the summer came back to her throat every day. At noon once, she went out for no particular reason and walked along the park, now closed. Behind the bare trees she could make out the line of the water tower which was giving off smoke. The banks had disappeared under the snow, now it looked like Ervant's village, the one he never mentioned anymore, which in winter resembled scenes in picture books, with the only breath coming from chimneys. Corrine wouldn't have gone back there, to contend with the frost and a badly ploughed road. She took what was within her reach.

But at noon hour the warm places where she might find her were closed, or deserted. In the main room of the Union Hotel there would be two or three solitary drinkers and a man washing the floor who would stare or insult her. There would be no Corrine, she would still be sleeping upstairs. She must ask someone, but who? A caretaker in slippers who would take her for a social worker, an informer who needed something to spy on? Her hair was loose and it fell freely to the beaver collar of a heavy navy wool coat, her tawny leather boots were freshly polished. A schoolteacher on the doorstep of a tavern.

Several times she was in the vicinity, buying a paper from the newsstand across the street, browsing in a store she'd never been to, going to the bank from which she could observe the front of the hotel, the ladies' entrance now blocked by the snow, and the storm door whose window was opaque with dirt. The street was bright, there really was no one walking past, but the whole town would see her go in.

She finally decided one Wednesday at five o'clock, when it was snowing and dark. There was no counter, no board with keys, no grimy manager. A bar where a boy in a black shirt was tidying up; he smiled at her. "Looking for the phone booth?" The few drinkers already at tables were watching television, the beery smell created a gentle warmth in the dimness, it was so simple, she discovered. She asked for Corrine, her room number, she could take the stairs on the left that led directly to the room. But would she recognize her? Or laugh? Or greet her briefly, indifferently, then send her away.

"Corrine? She isn't here any more. They left weeks ago." The boy was curious. He looked at Marie and he didn't go back to his glasses.

Thirteen

ACCORDING TO THE BOY, THEY HAD taken an apartment in town. He didn't know where. Their life at the hotel had become unbearable. Pietro rarely left his room, they couldn't even clean it, now and then, he'd fly into a rage, pound the wall at the slightest sound. He never went downstairs except to force Corrine to go up, in the middle of the night. "He's psychotic, you know."

The boy, the owner's son, was at the age to be studying social sciences. He mentioned it because they were both incongruous here, he in his almost clerical garb, she in her well-cut coat, and also because he wanted to keep her here for a moment. She could have claimed to be Corrine's cousin or a childhood friend. Say that they'd lost track of each other, that she had conducted a lengthy search before coming here. Talk with him about living in some hovel when luck has passed you by, and the country, vast as it is, is basically so small for human beings and has so little to offer the poor.

But she invented nothing in a story that boiled down to so little. She had met Corrine last summer, Pietro had been sick, they'd talked just like that, in a park, and with marriage, moving, travelling, going back to school, they'd got out of touch. She'd come to catch up, now that winter was here to stay, and she'd been able to find the time. It would soon be Christmas. Had she not left an address? "No," he said, "but I can ask."

He walked her to the door. Under his eyes he had a peculiar square ridge, it stood out very clearly on his pale face, exposed by his close-cropped hair. He repeated his promise to look. She promised to come back. Soon.

It was a Monday, and he behaved as if he'd been expecting her. He took her coat, seated her at the bar, offered her a beer which she refused because of the smell and because of Ervant later, offered her a coffee which she barely touched because of the faded cup. He didn't know exactly where Corrine lived now, but she was working in the little grocery store at the corner of Rhéaume. Marie said nothing, wanted not to believe him, but he had his theories. About women who aren't as strong as they seem, who dominate the weak, a common characteristic in a nation that is itself subservient. People raised their heads only to find out when to lower them under blackmail. Running a grocery store had always been a job for immigrants, who served there before going on to be served, and you could be an immigrant in your own country. For someone Corrine's age, though, it was the end of the road. At forty she would wear flowered dresses and an apron, and then Pietro would be able to sneer at her as well as tyrannize her.

He tried to make her shed the image of Corrine the survivor, the thistle. He gestured with his hands and brushed against her, but it was with words that he tried to get her on his side. There was no need to spar with her, she'd have been easy to take. Now that she had crossed the threshold it would have been good to go up to a room with him, spread a clean sheet, let herself be penetrated while she breathed in the musk of damp walls and of the long neck of this tense young man. There was a sensation of warmth in her groin, but he was looking at her like a girl you take to the movies and then to the Paris Café, a girl to be slept with only by candlelight and to music by Schumann, many weeks after the first kiss. What would Corrine have done to capture him?

She went out into a night filled with wind that lashed her under the layers of wool. She was five minutes from Corrine, from the grocery store that would be closed by the time she got there. She knew it well, it was the grocery store of her childhood, of errands done with bad grace. A place that smelled of canned goods, of stale apples, of cold meat at the back. A sleepy place where you only went when you had to, for a loaf of bread or a quart of milk. Marie remembered the grey cat, always in motion, that drove the mice towards the warehouse next door. She'd never been back.

But now she had no choice. She went along the main street that led directly there, the one she'd taken

thousands of times between school and home. She could
no longer travel it with her eyes shut. Everywhere service
stations had replaced the old apartment blocks, taverns,
restaurants, beauty parlours with apartments upstairs.
The town had always been ugly, now it was becoming
hideous. A harsh light fell onto snow mixed with oil, the
few trees had given way to garage billboards, there was
not a living soul except for vulgar men around their cars,
and two stray dogs that sniffed at one another.

She moved quickly, into the trap. Never had the shadows felt so close. There was nothing here now to erase
her anger and her isolation. She had expected to be able
to borrow from others their notions of elsewhere, to
steep herself in their images and to break up her own,
to triumph day by day over those who had narrowed
these hard places, places of evil spells, of rocks and
burns. But they had won, those who put up new
churches and gave streets the names of monsignors.
Their wind rose from the earth, it meandered through
their boundaries, whistled across her skin and made it
blotchy, it took her apart, and delivered her finally to
their small businesses, her culmination.

She had taken whatever she could from Ervant, who
had been able to live with ruptures, who had stubborn-
ly consumed them all. But she was wrong, he had
evolved instead from desertions to renunciations, driven
here by his fear of the past and ready now to settle
down in turn, to eat away a little more from this earth
of rust and metal, to plant some grass and a child that
resembles him, to keep his wife clean and to grab a
piece of any passing ass.

She had never had girlfriends, so inane were the girls in the convents and the wives of others you meet when you're twenty. But she'd had Corrine, so late it was already in pieces, scraps of history, scraps of bodies, scraps of summer. She knew very well what she had wanted: to slip into the nights of a woman who does not dream. Who laughs at the fearful and at the thousand subtle shades invented by feelings to hold you back, to turn girls into whimperers and later into women who lie in wait.

She was cutting, Corrine, and now the boy from the tavern who claimed to know everything had told the truth. She was cutting when she didn't belong to someone else, who kept her warm.

Marie would go there directly, to see that and to understand it. It would be two minutes to six, she would push open the door whose latch set off the two-note bell, she would meet a little girl carrying a paper bag, who would turn left near the middle of the hill. She might even be Diane, who was of no interest to her now.

She was going to see Corrine between the cans of soup and the cookie stand. She would pretend to have come here by chance, feign surprise at seeing her. They would exchange a few words about Pietro's illness, which was curable, and about her own more peaceful life. She'd buy her milk or her bread as she'd done in the past. In any event, that's what brings you here at six o'clock.

But it was from the cold room at the back that Corrine emerged. The metal door creaked on its hinges, she wore a white smock over black slacks. She looked the same but rounder, her face softer around eyelids that were still overly made-up. Marie didn't understand.

Corrine greeted her, laughing, took a long time to clean the big empty refrigerator, then she switched off the lights and went to the front to close up. She pulled a stool up to the cash drawer which had to be counted, and leaned on her elbows briefly to look at her. "I'm pregnant," she said. A radio at the end of the counter droned the sports news.

Fourteen

NO ONE WOULD EVER KNOW WHERE THE child had come from, the child she dared not kill. Pietro had wanted it furiously, thought it was his, from him. He saw a fence around the aging womb, and from that cage would be born a dark-haired girl with the curly head of southern Italy, whom he would one day show off while the cousins looked on. She would wear a dress as yellow as the sun, in a town square covered with dust.

It was a boy with tawny hair, and his ivory complexion would make him a local man. Pietro saw him once, his face impenetrable, eyes closed on the secret, motionless in a refusal that was not sleep. This creature had been forged between the thighs of a woman who had shunned his seed before accepting others, he forebade the child any journey out, any return. He had broken the cage and there would be no other.

This time Pietro would be discovered, twice dead, first poisoned, then drowned in the lake that washed him back to shore, just one more piece of trash.

The start of summer. The women saw that the child's eyes would be reddish-brown. He gave off an odour of acid that they would smell on their own skin long after. They gave him no name because they knew none for a child of that race, one who was made of lime and flint.

Very early he had the powerful breath of those beings whose lives will be long. He murmured cries without tears, a language of his own, carved from the very silence that others would maintain as they approached him.

Corrine feared the curse that was every day more present in the child's sandy eyes. First her breasts dried up, then her throat. Small creases formed at the edge of her shoulders, she thought she saw the bones peek through under the friable flesh. She would be the desert from which only scorpions emerged, now that she had driven away the animal of all her nights. No shadows now, no games, she would be an old woman and a child would reduce her to its own bright space. The paper came away from the walls, there were fires under the floors, and warnings that condemned the house. The neighbours left, she stayed behind, alone; in July the block would be razed.

Marie hovered over the child, serene. She put honey in his milk and answered his cries with phrases that, in the end, were stories. Wherein one could drink salt and eat oils, crush serpents and cast stones. Everything was possible in stories that no one but they would dare to know.

At three o'clock, on a day of brilliant sunshine, they went back to the park. Under a tree a radio was shrieking, a number of them were jumping around, young and pale. Two nearly naked girls danced on the moss. A languor fell like soot and drove them away, with the child, to where the burned stones were.

Nothing moved now in the undergrowth or along rocks dry to their roots. Not a dog. Muffled pounding came from the water tower, a mirage that quivered deep inside the light. "They're tearing it down," says Corrine. How does she know? From the child, a cry, softly.

It was then that Marie saw the lake, its rust marbled now with mauve water weeds that sprang from new crevices. The meeting with Isis. "It's midnight in the middle of day, the moons devour you alive, your blood will wet the stone for all eternity, reeds will grow from it. Ivy. Bonds. Lilacs bred of dead waters. The wound would be nothing, she had said, this woman whose shadow still covers your ankles. Her bones jut out now, they cut, they tear. She has no saliva. And you, you will flow forever."

The scar turned pink in the sun. "You remember," says the rasping voice. She didn't expect a reply. She said that she'd leave soon, go north where her thirst would be quenched, to the ice and cold the child would need, to be like the others. Here, fevers consume him. For the first time she was afraid. "I should have killed him, I told you I'd kill him."

A brown toad zigzagged between their legs. They had mistaken it for a stone.

Fifteen

WHERE THIS COUNTRY ENDS THERE IS no road, for all roads lead there. Ervant goes unburdened now, relieved of all the traces he dragged here, to the beginning of the world. Everything he has will not last for a thousand years, as it would over there, where his letters no longer arrive. Not his wife, not his house. His children will be born without memory, he will give them the music of metal and if he has a daughter she will have short hair. He has won this victorious place. The subsoil dies, neons reach to the gates of the city, to the rooftops of new motels where women lie down who can be seen in the offices, too.

He will not know about Marie's departure, she will remain. She smiles, she is getting ready to stay. After the house there will be a car, for trips to New York and the return, the fence around the garden will be fibreglass, the windows triple. A boat, some day, once the marina has been built at the base of the old water tower, and a pier with a bicycle path to the point. It's been announced next summer the work will begin.

At noon, alone, she goes towards the hills. It's easy to walk there, they are bare and no one comes because of the smell from the swamps on the western slope, where ferrous water from the mine stagnates. There is only undergrowth without a tree, feet creak on branches dead for years before the arrival of men, when the sun set fire to the useless trees. Their ashes would make a bed for a child of the embers, now gone. He would hear the crackling sound of dying bees. No flowers, no sap, they fall sputtering into the mud, the way we would like to depart, laughing.

The pavement whistles under cars come from the west. The first beasts of burden in this place were men, already shut up in their carcasses. They have brought the road with them and finished it here, where they met other men like themselves, come from the east. As a child she had thought she could lose herself here, but the boundaries are never far. She had only to skirt the swamps to find her reference point. You do not leave, do not learn how to lose yourself, in a prison. Barely time enough for touching terror, which was neither hot nor cold.

It is enough to dismantle desires, fling them to the bottom of the marsh, inspirations that she almost recognized, they plummet under the weight of a summer of rocks. They make bubbles. They rise up nowhere. Their shimmering dots the sky.

A census taker has climbed all the steps, descended all the

hollow roads. The count is untrue. Too many children

with ivory skin and tawny hair are born, have

disappeared. The town is closed, it is strewn with scraps of

them. Everything is asphalt, as far as the lamps. Impatient

women urge the seasons, which change on dusty squares.

Here there was once gold, and water, and men stirred the

earth. They wrote their names in mauve ink that welled

from the lake. A line races across the paper. Who turned it

yellow? The account is untrue.